# Cry, Baby

**"** Hi, Diary! I'm Charlie (short for Charlotte, which I hate). I'm fifteen-and-a-half. In my final year at lousy old school – hooray!

I'm going to tell you everything that happens to me – fill you up. It's going to be a fantastic year, I just know it. Here goes then. **"**

SHADES 2.0

# Cry, Baby

## Jill Atkins

Ransom

**SHADES 2.0**
Cry, Baby
by Jill Atkins

Published by Ransom Publishing Ltd.
Radley House, 8 St. Cross Road, Winchester, Hampshire SO23 9HX, UK
**www.ransom.co.uk**

ISBN      978 178127 187 2
First published in 2005
This updated edition published by Ransom Publishing 2013

# CONTENTS

*Tuesday 1st*
Hi, Diary! I'm Charlie (short for Charlotte, which I hate). I'm fifteen-and-a-half. In my final year at lousy old school – hooray!

I'm going to tell you everything that happens to me – fill you up. It's going to be a fantastic year, I just know it. Here goes then.

Had great time at party at Ellie's last night. Got home about four o'clock. Can't believe I saw the New Year in snogging Tom. Don't even fancy him! Must have been the booze, not that I was drunk (not really!!!) Just a bit tiddly. Got a bit of a hangover today. Mum says serves me right.

It's Danny I fancy. Trouble is, so does everyone else. Not surprising really, seeing how drop-dead gorgeous he is. He was there last night, but didn't speak to him, just couldn't keep my eyes off him. He looked at me once and winked, but think he does that to all the girls. I don't stand a chance. He doesn't normally go for small, dark-haired girls like me. Next time, I'll make more effort – you never know your luck! Mind you, he's got a reputation. Boys in my class say he's slept with half the girls in town. Not this half though!

*Wednesday 2nd*
It's Katie's 16th next Saturday. She's having a party. She's invited Danny!

Boring day, doing nothing much.

What shall I wear on Sat? Wonder if I can get a new outfit out of Mum.


*Thursday 3rd*
Dragged Mum to the Sales – bought stunning new skirt and top. Really sexy. Dad says the skirt's too short and the top's too tight, but he's so *boring*.


*Friday 4th*
Katie's party tomorrow. Took some of my Christmas money and bought some new make-up. Ellie came round. Practised making each other's faces up. Good laugh!

*Saturday 5th*

Tonight's the night! Got butterflies – so excited. Danny can't miss me with my new look. He'll be bowled over with my ravishing beauty!!! Not!

Ellie's coming round at six so we can get ready.

Dad keeps on about girls growing up too fast these days (his words). Says I'm a recipe for disaster if I tart myself up (his words) for any over-sexed male to take advantage of (his words again). Told him to get a life, move into the twenty-first century. Can look after myself.


*Sunday 6th*

It happened – was more than a bit drunk, so can't remember much.

Party began well. Everyone said I looked great. Tom wanted to snog again, but kept myself off him. Didn't want to ruin my make-up, or my chances. Kept dancing, tried to stay as near to Danny as poss all the time, let him see me dance. I'm a good mover, got good rhythm.

Katie had made an enormous bowl of punch – dread to think what was in it. Must have been potent. Began to feel free as air, then head started to spin, arms and legs didn't really belong to me. Felt great!

Suddenly, Danny's dancing beside me. Nearly passed out with excitement. He was staring at me. Felt his eyes all over me. He got closer and closer, in and out of focus.

Next minute, was in his arms. Felt his hands round my waist first, then all over. And kissing? Never been kissed like that before! Like he was eating me.

Shock, thrill? Was in heaven. To think that Danny had noticed me – fancied little old me! Kissed him back, and how!

Next thing I know, he's pulling me through the crowd, into the hall in Katie's house, up the stairs.

Head's reeling, see a bed, Katie's bed, covered in coats and stuff. Danny pushes them off and shoves me down. Head spins, feel rather numb. There seems like two of him, then one. Then he's down on top of me.

A while later, I'm lying there. Danny's gone. Try and move, but can't. Body weighs a tonne, head belongs to someone else, arms limp, legs ache. What did we do? Can't remember. Only him, heavy on top. Pain. Yes, pain, remember that.

Must have done it! So that was *it*? Where was the fantastic sensation you were supposed to feel?

Managed to get up. Staggered to the

bathroom. Sat on the loo, head still reeling.

Then looked in the mirror. What a sight! Then sick down the loo. Tidied myself up. Crept back to Katie's room and lay on the bed. Ellie found me there. Said I'd got a headache. Can't tell her the truth. Not until got head round what happened.

Feel bad today. And sore. Not how imagined it would be. Wish hadn't been such an easy lay. Even with Danny. Still, now he's my bloke. Next time we meet, I'll play it cool.

Wonder if he'll ring me today. He can easily find my number – it's in the book.

Monday 7th
Back to school today. Everyone full of Katie's party. All had fantastic time. Except me. Kept quiet all day.

Waited in all evening. Danny didn't ring.

Been thinking – terrifying thoughts keep going round and round in my head.

Supposing … What if … ? It was what they call 'unprotected' sex. Could have caught something off him. Could be pregnant! Oh, God!

Can't talk to Mum or Dad about it. They'd take off into orbit. Nor Ellie. She likes boys, but won't give herself away. Not like I did. No one would understand.

*Monday 14th*
Haven't written anything for a whole week.

Nothing's happened, that's why. Feeling too depressed. Kind of scared, screwed up inside.

Exams started today. Mocks. Couldn't concentrate.

Danny – he's a pig – never did ring. Tried to get his number, but it was impossible.

Can't get thoughts to go away. Mum says I've become an old misery. Blamed exams, but she's right.

*Tuesday 15th*
Still nothing. Given up on Danny ringing. He must be laughing – *pathetic female*, he'll think. Or worse still, he'll have forgotten all about me by now – Charlie who?

More exams. Definitely failed.

*Saturday 19th*
Saw Danny last night. Outside the burger bar, arms round some tall blonde. I hate her. Hate him. Hate all boys. Keeping away from them from now on.

Ellie asked why I'm not going out tonight. Lied. Said I had to visit the grandparents.

*Saturday 26th*
Saturday again. Got invited to another party. Not going. Can't face the chance of meeting Danny and *her*. Anyway, feel a bit off today. And my period's late.

*Sunday 27th*
Didn't want any breakfast. Pretended to eat some toast. Threw it in the bin.

My brain's gone on frozen mode. Keeps going over and over the same thing.

Can't be pregnant, can I? Not after one lousy experience.

Hardly slept a wink last night. Brain racing. What if I *am* pregnant?

*Thursday 31st*
Met Danny face to face in the street. Couldn't avoid him. Did a damn foolish thing. Burst into tears, blubbered all over

the place. Hinted I thought I could be
pregnant.

He just laughed. Asked me who the
father was – told me to be more careful
next time. *Me* be more careful? Could kill
him.

# FEBRUARY

*Friday 1st*

Exams finished. Dread results.

Going mad with worry. Still no sign of a period. And was sick this morning, really sick, down the loo. That's got to confirm it. Must get a test.

*Saturday 2nd*

I can't be, I can't be, I can't be. It's not fair, it's just not fair!

Well, that's it then. Test positive! Feel desperate. Want to scream! What am I going to do? Leave home? I'll have to. Can't face telling anyone.

Got a pregnancy test this morning. Not from the local chemist. Word might get around. Caught the bus to Haselbury. Waited hours before daring to go in and ask. Had to be the young one served me. Even she gave me the eye.

Came home, shaking like a leaf. Shut myself in the bathroom and did the test. Spent so long in there, Dad banged on the door. He'll throw me out, I know he will. Oh, God! I'm such a stupid idiot! If only I could turn the clock back …

*Sunday 3rd*

Sick several times. Feel as if my guts are turning inside out. Have to try and do it quietly. Have to act OK. Been putting blusher on, hide my ghostly pale cheeks.

Went round to Ellie's. She asked me several times if I was all right. Lost my temper with her. Not like me at all. Maybe she suspects. Should I tell her?

*Monday 4th*

School was hell. Had to skip a couple of lessons. Spent hours with head down loo.

Stinking place made me feel loads worse. Ellie keeps staring at me. I know she knows.

*Saturday 9th*

Ellie knows. Actually, she made a few hints. Then she came right out with it.

'You pregnant?' she asks.

Swore her to secrecy. Told her everything. Felt better in a way. Talked for hours in my room.

'Why didn't you take a morning-after pill?' she asks. Said I didn't know why – probably too numb.

'And too *dumb*,' she says. Says I need my brains testing. Too late now – you have to take them soon after.

'Get rid of it,' she says. 'There's no way you could have a baby.' (No, can't imagine that in a million years) 'I'll ask my sister what you should do.'

Ellie's sister Megan's eighteen.

Thought of abortion makes me absolutely petrified. But at least then Mum and Dad never get to find out.


*Wednesday 13th*
I hate this baby. Why did it have to come

21

and disturb my life? Refuse to think about it as anything but a thing.

Hate Danny, too, for what he's done to me.

Made appointment to see the doctor. Got to wait nearly a week!! That's the trouble with wanting to see the lady doctor – there's no way I could see a man.

*Monday 18th*
Saw Dr Owen today. Luckily it's half term, so didn't have to bunk off. Mum and Dad were at work.

Dr Owen was really nice. My legs felt weak as water when I went in. She kind of guessed why I'd come. Promised it would be a secret between us. Told me doctors have to sign an oath saying they'll never tell any patients' business to anyone – even parents!

Jumped right in. 'I hate this thing, want

22

an abortion,' I said, pretending to be hard. Wanted her to think I don't care. Trouble is, I think I do. Couldn't stop bawling my eyes out.

She's so calm, and kind. Handed me a tissue. Asked me when it happened. Wasn't judgemental at all. Then asked when was my last period? It was Christmas Eve. Had stomach cramps all over Christmas – great!

Worked out how far gone I am. Eight weeks. Baby would be due October 1st.

Refuse to think about that. It, thing, nothing more. Going to get rid of it.

'Do your parents know?' she asks.

'Not on your life,' I say.

She told me abortion might be possible, but must think of the options first. Told her I knew them. She reminded me anyway.

- Have the baby and keep it. She says lots of girls do these days.

- Have the baby adopted. More common in my gran's day.
- Have an abortion. Can be done, have to get two doctors to say it's necessary on mental health grounds.

Said again I want abortion.

She smiled, then said she wanted me to think about it for a few days, come back and see her on Friday. (Friday? That's four whole days I've got to wait.)

What is there to think about?

'Think how you would feel afterwards,' she says. 'Each time you see a baby, in the supermarket, in the street, anywhere, would you wish it was yours? On the day it was due to be born or on an anniversary, would you regret getting rid of it? Would you wish it was there to love?'

'I'd feel OK,' I say.

'Well, think about it anyway,' she says. 'If

you're still sure on Friday, we can look into doing it. Best done before twelve weeks, otherwise it gets more difficult and complicated.'

Stood up to leave.

Then she says. 'Why don't you tell your parents? It's not easy to go through an abortion.' And if I change my mind about the abortion (which I won't) they'd have to know eventually.

Said I'd think about it. How can I tell them, though? They'll murder me.

*Tuesday 19th*
Keep being horribly sick. Have to be careful. Mum's noticed something. Asked me if I'm all right. Nearly blabbed then almost fainted with terror. Mouth totally dry, brain in a panic.

Will I ever dare tell her? Definitely *not*

going to tell them both at once. Maybe get Mum on her own in a good mood. Not today, though.

Went to Ellie's. Told her about Dr Owen. Ellie says, 'What is there to think about?'

Megan says they should give me an abortion without any bother. How does she know?

*Wednesday 20th*
Keep looking at myself in the mirror. Do I show yet? Course not! Baby's only teeny tiny at the moment. Learnt that in biology. Easier to abort.

Set me thinking though. That's a baby in there.

Stopped myself. It's a thing, nothing, a silly mistake. Soon to be gone.

Went to cinema with Ellie and Katie.

Katie kept looking at my stomach. Has

Ellie told her, the cow? She promised not to breathe a word, but hasn't signed an oath like the doctor.

Chickened out of telling Mum again.

What am I going to say to Dr Owen? Thought it would be easy, but can't make up my mind. Keep seeing babies, like she said. They look so cute. And loveable. But that's other people having them, not me. Not me. Certainly not me.

Get rid of it, I keep saying to myself. It's not a person.

Or is it? When do babies become people?

*Thursday 21st*
What a day! Well actually, what a nightmare!

Mum caught me being sick down the loo.

Collared me afterwards. Sat me down in the kitchen.

'Well?' she says. 'Have you got something you ought to be telling me?'

Wished for an earthquake or a thunderbolt, but it didn't happen. Swallowed hard, fought off the need to be sick and faint at the same time. Saw dragon face of Mum waiting to breathe fire over me. Came over all hot without that.

Burst into tears, couldn't help it.

'It's no use trying to get my sympathy,' she says, 'especially if I've guessed right. You're pregnant, aren't you? How far gone?'

That set me off again. I'm just a kid.

'Eight-and-a-half weeks. I'm sorry. It was only once,' I sobbed. 'At a party. It just happened.'

'Just happened?' she shouts so loud I could hear the glasses in the cupboard pinging. 'Sorry? You will be! After *all* we've given you, you throw this in our faces. Our only daughter … '

So I told her everything, like I'd told Ellie. About the punch Katie had mixed and Danny (though I didn't say his name) and the pain and the not knowing what I was doing.

She was pacing the floor, steaming, not speaking.

'What are we going to tell your father?' she says at last. 'He was right, wasn't he? Laying yourself open to an over-sexed male. He'll give me hell for this, you realise that, young lady? You'll have to get rid of it.'

She ranted on for ages. No mention of how I might be feeling or about what rotten luck to get pregnant after one time.

Didn't eat all day, couldn't sit still, had to get out of the house. Wandered round town, trying to avoid babies. Didn't manage that, though. Never noticed so many before. Dreaded Dad coming home.

But he got me fainting from shock. When Mum (who hadn't said a word to me the rest of the day) told him, he was silent for several minutes. Then he hugged me.

'Poor old Charlie,' he says.

Why do parents always surprise you like that?

*Friday 22nd*
*Morning* – Today's the day. Have to make a decision. Never found anything so difficult before in my whole life.

After I wrote my diary last night, Dad came up to my room. Said I'd better come downstairs again so we could talk. Mum was still ranting away. Dad said things like, 'You were young once,' and 'Don't be too harsh on the poor girl. She must be going through it.' Just the opposite to before.

Mum eventually calmed down. She hugged me, too. Then we all cried. Never seen Dad cry before. Dead weird. Then he asked who had done this to me. Wants to beat him up. As if that would help!

Refused to say Danny's name. It's not important any more. Told them I was going to get an abortion.

'For the best,' they both said, then I went back to bed.

Best for who? I kept wondering. Not best for the baby that's growing inside, that's for sure! Poor little thing. Wonder if it's a boy or a girl? What would I call it?

Had to stop myself again. What am I thinking of? It doesn't matter what it is, does it? Or does it? Is it right to do away with it, as if it's any old bit of rubbish?

*Later* – Was in with Dr Owen for hours. Glad Mum and Dad weren't there. Needed to tell doctor about what they had said. Had to be able to think straight.

Haven't made a final decision yet. Too many questions unanswered in my head. Don't seem to hate it any more.

Dr Owen was brilliant. Said she could only give me facts and general advice, but it had to come from me. I'm nearly nine weeks gone. I can have another week or so, go back and see her when I'm ready. If I decide to keep the baby, she'll make arrangements for a scan at twelve weeks.

Keep the baby? Should I?

*Sunday 24th*
Ellie's really giving me a hard time. Can't believe I haven't gone through with it yet. How can she know what's the right thing to

do? Don't like her attitude any more. Thinks she can run my life.

*Monday 25th*
Oh my God! I'd forgotten the exams. Brain has been on other things! Results so far: Maths, History, French, all bad. Teachers were mad. I couldn't give true reason. How will I add this to Mum and Dad's worries?

*Tuesday 26th*
More of the same. Highest mark was English Lit. I'll tell Mum and Dad tomorrow.

Well, Baby, what am I going to do about you?

*Wednesday 27th*
Was putting off telling them about the exams, but Dad asked me. Had to tell him. No point in lying. They'd find out soon

enough at Parents' Evening in a couple of weeks.

Feel really guilty, though. Dad looked so disappointed. He knows I'm not that bad. He wants me to go to Uni, but I'm not so sure.

Wonder what you look like, Baby. If I just wait until after the scan, just so I can see you. But then you'll be more than twelve weeks. Is that too late? I'll ask Dr Owen.

*Friday 1st*

Been to see Dr Owen again. Told her I was having trouble deciding. Can't bring myself to get rid of it. Think I'm beginning to feel attached to it. Realise I've started talking to it. Think I want to keep it.

She says, in that case, she'll go ahead and arrange a scan. If I change my mind, I can always come back.

Wow! Head's in a spin. A scan. In two weeks I'll see you, Baby.

Feel lousy all the time. Can she give me anything for sickness? She says find something I can eat that doesn't make me sick and stick to that for the time being. Doesn't like giving out drugs to pregnant women.

Mum and Dad still think I'm going to get rid of you, Baby. Have to tell them tomorrow.

*Saturday 2nd*
Told them. Mum cried a lot. Dad looked like a dog whose bone had been snatched away from him. What about my education?

I said I could do it later.

How do I feel, now I've made up my mind? Brilliant! Apart from puking all the time and wanting to sleep.

I'm going to keep you, Baby. Can't wait

to meet you!

October 1st. That's such a long way off!

*Monday 4th*
French bread does the trick. Managed to eat some and it stayed down.

*Wednesday 6th*
Just had Parents' Evening. Mum and Dad didn't look too happy when they came home. Have appointment to see the Head tomorrow after school.

*Thursday 7th*
Went to Mrs Dobson's office at four-thirty. Mrs D looked like she'd taken very nasty medicine when Dad told her the news. Looked at me as if I was the horrible person who had forced her to take it. Which I am, I suppose.

Mum and Dad didn't look a lot better.

Had big chat when we got home. They want me to make effort with GCSEs. They say, might as well get good results if I can. Promised to do my best.

I'll do it for you, Baby.


*Saturday 9th*

Went to party. News is out. They all know, but spent most of the time being sick so they would have guessed anyway. Danny was there. Don't care any more. Dad says he's not worth it.

Ellie thinks I'm mad. Probably am!


*Saturday 16th*

The magic twelve weeks! Scan's on Monday.

Not done much this week.

School, eating french bread, trying not to be sick, homework.

*Monday 18th*

You're beautiful, Baby! Absolutely fantastic! I'm in love!

Strange experience, having a scan. Not good at first. Felt sick as usual and petrified. Got the shakes on the way to the hospital. Mum's come round a bit. Glad she was there.

Then jelly on my belly and a freezing cold nozzle. Watched the screen. Saw blobs, then a shape that looked a bit like a frog.

'That's it,' says the lady.

'I'm having a frog!' I say. Then I saw it move.

I saw you move, Baby! Could see you weren't a frog. You've got dear little arms and legs and a head and body. Couldn't see you clearly, but I know you're there. Got a photo of you. Black and white, very blurry, but it's you.

*Tuesday 19th*
Dr Owen says all is going well.

*Friday 22nd*
Had blood test this morning, check I'm not anaemic.

Beginning to feel much better. Must be because I'm into the second trimester (Dr Owen said.) Got a little bit of a pot-belly.

*Tuesday 26th*
End of term coming up in a couple of weeks. Teachers all know about me now. Some are OK, others look like they've got a bad smell under the nose. All nagging me to work hard for exams next term.

Ellie's been nicer, coming round to the idea of the baby. Gives me big hugs, pats my belly. Big relief for me. Hated being split from her. Katie's great, too, but her mum's a bit anti. (Cold fish.) Does she know it happened in her house?

Keep looking at the photo. My baby! Doesn't seem real. Can't imagine what it will be like being a mum.

Are you a boy or girl, Baby? I'm dying to know. October seems so long to wait.

*Saturday 30th*
Great day! Shopping with Ellie and Mum. Bought new trousers and skirt. Can't get the waist done up on any of my clothes. Seem to be getting larger day by day.

That's you, making this bump, Baby. Couldn't resist buying you a little teddy. Silly, I know!

*Monday 1st*
Have decided I'm going to work for the exams. Who's the April Fool? Prob me!

Started eating again, without being sick, thank God. Gone off French bread.

*Friday 5th*
Blood test results good.

Finished school today. Hooray! Mum picked me up at the school gate. She'd bought me a new top, quite stylish, but plenty of room for expansion!

Think she feels sorry for me a bit. Believes me now it was only once. Blames the alcohol. Knows I made a big mistake.

Don't think of you as a mistake now, Baby. Part of me, going to be one of the family.

*Saturday 6th*

It was hell today. Had to tell Nan and Grandad. We're here for the weekend. Mum sat with me while I told them this afternoon. Could hear my voice squeaking and dying away. Hands felt sweaty. Head light, feet made of lead. Stuttered and spluttered. Finally managed to tell them how it had happened.

Grandad just said, 'Oh dear, my little sunflower.' (That's what he calls me.) He gave me a hug, but his eyes told me he was sad.

Felt so small. Wanted to tell him it wasn't true.

Nan went very pale then started muttering things like, 'In my day,' and 'What is the world coming to?' Does she hate me? She hasn't spoken to me since then.

Came to bed early. Needed to be on my own to cry.

*Monday 8th*
Glad to be back home. Mum says Nan will come round in the end.

Hope so. Nan did kiss me when we came away, but it wasn't her usual snuggly one.

Feel kind of empty and flat.

I want them to be happy about you, Baby.

Seen loads of babies around. And pregnant women. All shapes and sizes. Can't believe I'm going to get that big. Beginning to feel huge already.

*Thursday 11th*
Had a card from Nan and Grandad this morning. Really lovely. Gave me goose pimples all over. Said they were upset it had happened, but they know I'm a good girl. Said they'll always love me and my baby. Did it make me howl?!

(It might sound slushy, but I'm in that kind of mood. Must be my condition!)

Sent them a card back. It just said 'Thanks!' inside.

*Friday 12th*
Seeing loads of Ellie and Katie and a couple of others during the hols. All being v friendly.

They want to know what I'm going to call you, Baby. Haven't got any idea yet.

Katie bought one of those *Naming Your Baby* books. Couldn't believe some of the names in it! Had a great laugh!

*Wednesday 17th*
Did some French oral. Tested Ellie, then she tested me. Ended up rolling on the floor in fits of helpless laughter.

Went to see Dr Owen again. She prodded around a bit. Took my blood pressure. Says I'm doing fine. Got to book the hospital place. Met the midwife – she'll be keeping an eye on me from now on.

Feel really proud of my belly. I'm expanding fast, really show now.

Got thinking about names again. Thought Brad might be good for a boy, or Connor, but I'm not sure. Rosie or Polly for a girl. How do I know what will suit that little person in there?

What do you think, Baby?

*Saturday 20th*
Aunty Lizzie and Uncle Mark and Emma and James came round. They know, of course. Bet Mum was on the phone to Aunty Lizzie the moment she knew.

Emma wanted to know all about how I got pregnant. She's only twelve and I didn't know how much I was allowed to tell her. In the end I told her everything. She listened with her eyes popping out of their sockets.

'I thought you had to love someone to get pregnant,' she says.

Made me laugh, though I suppose I thought I was in love with Danny at the time.

*Monday 22nd*
Back at school today. Nag, nag, nag.
That's all the teachers do, but made myself
do some revision this evening. Might as
well try and get a few good grades.

*Tuesday 23rd*
Wow! Felt you move this evening, Baby.
Thought I'd got wind at first. Sort of bubbly
feeling inside. Then it happened again. The
third time, I suddenly twigged. It must be
you, Baby.

Couldn't wait to tell Ellie. Sent text to
her.

*Wednesday 24th*
Ellie said she was jealous of me when I
described feeling you move inside, Baby.

She's coming round every night from now
on.

*Wednesday 1st*
Baby's on the move.

*Saturday 4th*
Happy Birthday to me!

Mum and Dad gave me some more
clothes. Nan and Grandad sent me some
money and a book all about looking after a

baby. Got loads of cards.

Went out to pizza place with the crowd. Ate *so much* pizza. Eating for two.

Baby loved it, didn't you, Baby? You're so lively. Better call you Tigger, you bounce so much!

*Thursday 9th*
Almost twenty weeks, half-way.

Next week's a big week – second scan, see midwife at the clinic and French Oral.

*Monday 13th*
Second scan – that jelly and the cold nozzle again – ouch! Mind you, it was worth it.

You're gorgeous, Baby! And you've grown so much. Could see you much more clearly this time. You seemed to be waving your tiny little hand. Still don't know if you're a girl or a boy. Couldn't quite see the vital parts! Have to keep guessing.

*Tuesday 14th*
Had clinic appointment – blood pressure, urine test, etc. Midwife and doctor v pleased with scan. All normal.

Heard your heart beat, Little Baby. Very fast, twice as fast as mine. Must be because you're doing your exercises so much.

*Wednesday 15th*
Nan and Grandad came over. Nan says I'm carrying for a boy. I wonder if any of that's true?

Are you a boy, Baby?

*Friday 17th*
*Parlez–vous Francais?* Not a lot! Oral was a nightmare. Still, it's over and done with.

One down, about a hundred to go!

51

Going out tomorrow night to a disco. Last fling before exams.

You can dance inside, Baby, while I dance outside.

*Saturday 18th*
Ellie rang. She's ill. Some kind of virus. Hope it's nothing catching. She's hoping she'll have to miss the exams. Had fantastic time at disco. (Pity Ellie wasn't there).

*Monday 20th*
Ellie's still at death's door (according to her on the phone).

Baby's really lively. Belly's expanding.

*Saturday 25th*
Ellie's better. She's cursing. Can't get out of the exams now – hee hee!

No time to write. Been studying hard.

*Monday 3rd*
Went in for first exam.

Found it uncomfortable sitting still for two hours. Kept having to shift in my chair. Teacher let me stand up for a few minutes and took me to the toilet, twice!

You were jumping up and down on my bladder, weren't you, Baby?

*Saturday 8th*
Thank God for Saturdays! Exams all week
– I'm dead whacked!

*Tuesday 11th*
Clinic again today. I'm twenty-four weeks
now. Everything going fine. Baby's heartbeat
was 155 to the minute. Nan says that
means a girl. I wish she'd make up her
mind!

I don't mind what you are, Baby. Have I
really got to wait till October?

No more writing in this diary until exams
are over. Haven't got time.

*Friday 21st*
Hooray! Last exam was today. Don't think
I've done too badly.

Crowd went down to pizza place to
celebrate. Got indigestion now. Serves me

right for being such a piggy.

Baby kicking my stomach! Going to be a footballer?

*Sunday 23rd*
Didn't notice until this evening (was too busy with Aunty Lizzie and the rest here – Emma never left me alone for a second), but the baby doesn't seem to be leaping around as usual.

*Monday 24th*
*Morning* – Sitting quietly writing, this morning, can't feel the baby moving at all.

Come on, Baby, time for gymnastics!

Normally, when I'm still, it's the most active. Is it just having a rest?

A bit worried. Should I tell Mum? Will she just say I'm making a fuss?

*Later* – Going to tell Mum. Feel uneasy. Baby's still not on the go.

*Later still* – Told Mum. She called Dr Owen.
   Waiting for the ambulance now.
   Oh God, what's happening to me?
   What's wrong with my baby?

*Wednesday 26th*
Oh, Diary, I'm home now, but how can I write anything?
   How can I say how I feel?
   I've lost her. My baby!

*Thursday 27th*
Rushed to hospital that night, taken straight through emergency, into the labour ward.
   I was going mad. What was happening? Nobody said much, just kept asking me

when did I last feel the baby moving? Then they wired me up.

No sound. No fast heartbeat that I had begun to love. Only silence.

Clock ticking. Hollow footsteps along the corridor. Babies crying.

But no sound that I wanted to hear. Not my baby.

I saw that look in the nurse's eyes and I knew.

I felt totally frozen, locked in another world.

*I've lost you, Baby*, I kept hearing echoing inside my head.


*Friday 28th*
Had to go through labour. They induced me, a needle in the back of my hand, a drip.

Pains started suddenly, quickly, like fire burning me inside out.

Pain, coming in waves, crashing me against rocks.

Pain, over and over and over, all for nothing, knowing that my baby was dead.

She was a little girl, my baby. They let me see her, hold her for just a second before they took her away.

So tiny, so perfect. Part of myself. Lost, like myself.

I named her Rosie. Dad took a photo of her. It's on the bed beside me now. I keep looking at her, wishing.

Eyes tightly closed, fingers clenched, all blurred through my tears.

If only those tiny fingers could be holding my finger now!

What went wrong? Why did I have to lose you?

Oh, Rosie, why did you have to die?

*Saturday 29th*

Ellie came round. She thinks it's her fault. The baby caught her virus.

Couldn't face her. Sent her away. Can't face anyone.

If only I had told Mum when I first noticed, I could have saved Rosie.

I can't forgive myself. It was my fault!

I'm alone inside a cold, dark hole, dropping like a stone, falling deeper and deeper, going on forever. There's no end, no way out.

Dr Owen came. Turned my back on her, closed my ears to her voice, but she spoke to me anyway. Said it's not my fault, gave me some pills.

What I want to know is, why me? Why *my* baby?

*Monday 1st*
Had letter from Mrs Dobson. It said,
'Perhaps it was just as well, in the
circumstances.' How could she be so mean,
the stupid old bat? Ripped the letter into a
thousand pieces. I hate her.

Then got a card from a neighbour.
'You're young. There's plenty of time to

have more.' She doesn't know, does she, interfering old woman?

I don't want more. I only want Rosie.

I've been taking the pills, meant to stop me being depressed.

As if pills could do that.

Nothing can lift me out of this dark hole.

*Tuesday 2nd*

Dr Owen came again. Managed to face her today. She's so nice. Stayed with me for ages, talking.

She said I could have had an infection in my womb or a virus – apparently they're the most common reasons for losing a baby at this late stage.

I said I *knew* it was my fault.

She said it wasn't. Doctors don't understand enough about it yet to know how to stop it. It was just bad luck. But it's not likely to happen to me again.

Big deal! Doesn't help, knowing that.
Why should I have all the bad luck?

Then she showed me some exercises. Get
my muscles back to normal.

In the end, we talked about Rosie's
funeral – that's tomorrow.

Told her I couldn't bear to go.

She says I *need* to go. Need to say goodbye.


*Thursday 4th*

It's over. Empty, that's how I feel.

Funeral was awful. The flowers. That
little white coffin! I couldn't stop imagining
that tiny baby lying in there. Part of me.

I was a block of ice, rigid, shivering,
melting in tears.

Dad held me the whole time, trying to
comfort me.

He was crying, too. So were Mum and

Nan and Grandad. They must all care.

And Dr Owen, she was there. She was right. I'm glad I went.

Glad I could say goodbye to you, Baby.


*Monday 8th*

It's two weeks now. Been doing the exercises.

My stomach is slowly getting flatter.

Went out today, with Ellie. First time since …

Kept seeing babies, though, like Dr Owen said.

Wished they were mine.

I still cry for you, Baby. Still miss you. Guess I always will.

## Rising Tide

*by Anne Rooney*

When Chris finds Danny, he knows he's a *Runner* – a refugee running away from a country destroyed by climate change. Chris should hand Danny in to the authorities. That's what everyone else would do. But Chris feels differently. Will he risk his own future for the sake of his new friend?

## Hauntings

*by Mary Chapman*

It is Rebecca Jane's birthday, the first since her mum died. Dad eagerly gives her a present, but when Rebecca opens it she steps into a living nightmare. Has the Victorian sampler she has received unlocked a ghost from the past? How can Rebecca escape this restless ghost and its haunting power?